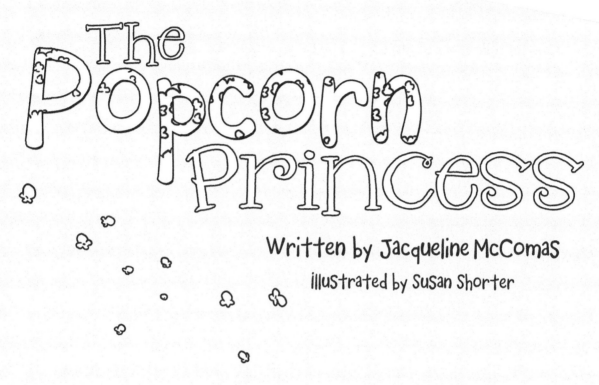

The Popcorn Princess

Written by Jacqueline McComas

illustrated by Susan Shorter

enchanting adventures of a little girl who loves yummy popcorn
and what happens when she keeps asking for more and more.

Archway Publishing books may be ordered through booksellers or by contacting:

Archway Publishing
1663 Liberty Drive
Bloomington, IN 47403
www.archwaypublishing.com
1 (888) 242-5904

ISBN: 978-1-4808-2631-1 (sc)
ISBN: 978-1-4808-2632-8 (e)

Print information available on the last page.

Archway Publishing rev. date: 1/29/2016

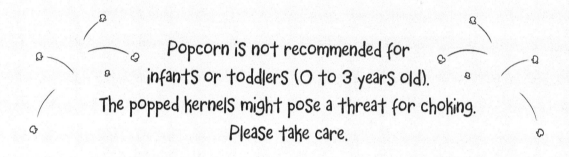

Popcorn is not recommended for infants or toddlers (0 to 3 years old). The popped kernels might pose a threat for choking. Please take care.

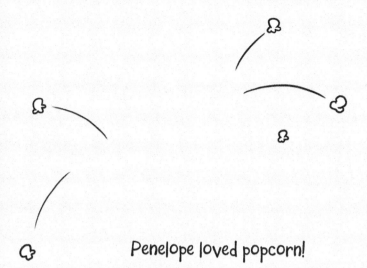

Penelope loved popcorn!

Most children say "da-da" or "ma-ma" when they first learn to talk. But not Penelope. Her first word was "popcorn."

She thought the popcorn popper was magical -- she looked in wonder as each puff of popcorn danced in the air.

Popcorn here, popcorn there, popcorn popping everywhere!

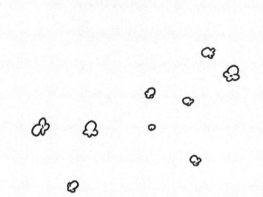

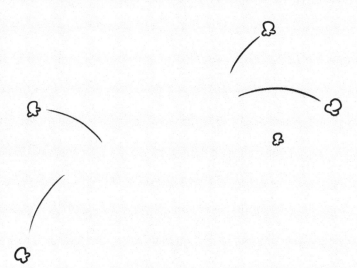

Penelope's wagon was filled with popcorn. Her fluffy
mattress, pillow, and quilt were filled with popcorn.

Penelope's mother and father started
to call her Popcorn Princess.

Popcorn here, popcorn there, popcorn popping everywhere!

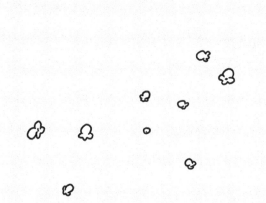

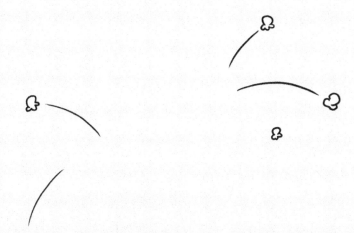

The playground at Penelope's was exciting and fun. all the boys and girls in the neighborhood would swing or slide into mountains of crunchy, munchy popcorn.

Others tossed creamy-caramel popcorn balls back and forth.

all her friends called her Popcorn Princess.

Popcorn here, popcorn there, popcorn popping everywhere!

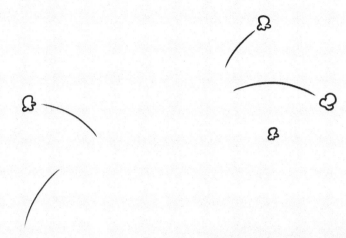

As Popcorn Princess grew older, she loved popcorn even more.

She filled her swimming pool with popcorn for splash parties.

Her guests enjoyed popcorn popperoni pizzas.
But, it was the popcorn popsicles that everyone
loved the most — so many delicious flavors.

Popcorn here, popcorn there, popcorn popping everywhere!

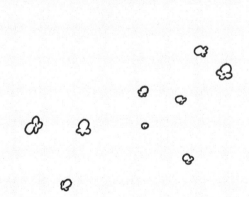

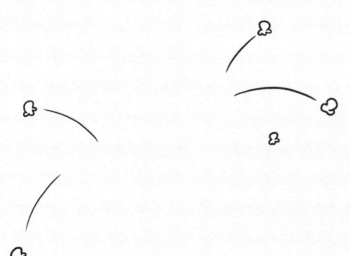

Popcorn Princess kept asking for more and more
popcorn. Every room in the house was filled with
popcorn. There was no room to walk.

Once her poodle Butterball was lost in a
pile of popcorn for a whole day.

Popcorn here, popcorn there, popcorn popping everywhere!

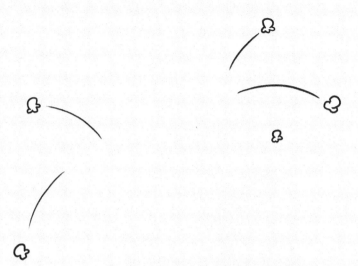

and then . . . all of a sudden . . . something happened.
There was just too much popcorn and . . . POP! The
whole house popped apart with a popping sound that
could be heard throughout the neighborhood.

everyone flew up, up into the air – Popcorn Princess,
her mother, her father, and even Butterball.

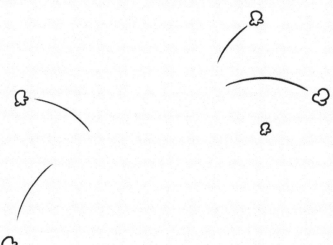

Luckily, everyone landed on soft, puffy piles of popcorn.

Penelope's mother and father shook off all the popcorn
from their clothes. They stood up and shouted to
Popcorn Princess, "NO MORE POPCORN!"

Popcorn Princess did not say a word. She thought
for a moment and then with a big smile said,

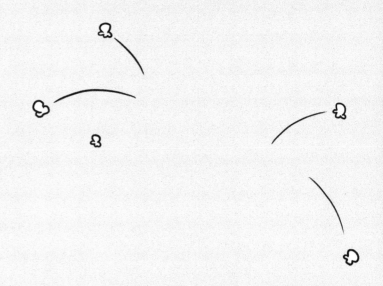

"How about cotton candy?"

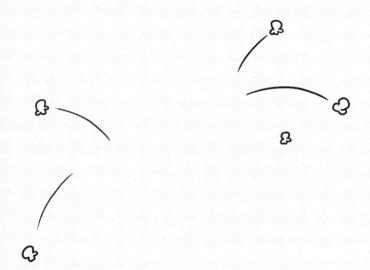

THE END

RECIPE

(Adult supervision is required)

POPCORN PRINCESS'S PARTY POPCORN

<u>Ingredients:</u>

6 cups of popcorn.

3 to 5 ounces melted white chocolate (add a teaspoon of shortening for easy drizzle).

Rainbow colored sprinkles or jimmies.

Place popcorn in large bowl or on cookie sheet.

Drizzle white chocolate over popcorn, sprinkle with colored jimmies, and toss.

eat at once or place in refrigerator to set. enjoy!

POPCORN FACTS

Popcorn is america's favorite snack food.

There are 2 shapes of popcorn: snowflake and mushroom.
The snowflake shape is usually sold at the movies because it is bigger.

The unpopped kernels are called Old Maids or Spinsters.

each kernel of popcorn has a tiny drop of water inside.
When it is heated, it explodes and pops inside out.

POPCORN ACTIVITIES

Make other words from this sentence: i love popcorn with butter.

Write a poem or sing a song using the word "popcorn."

Hang strings of popcorn made with a needle and thread
on tree branches or bushes for birds to eat.

Use paper, art supplies, and popcorn to create works of art.